T0128586

GOOD FRIENDS

Shirley Rogers Baustian

Library of Congress Control Number: 2016915465

ISBN: Softcover 978-1-5245-4392-1
Hardcover 978-1-5245-4393-8
EBook 978-1-5245-4391-4

Print information available on the last page

Rev. date: 10/04/2016

To order additional copies of this book, contact:
Xlibris
1-888-795-4274
www.Xlibris.com
Orders@Xlibris.com

DEDICATION

This book is dedicated to Leif Anderson. When we were visiting him and his wife Maud in Sweden, Leif looked out across a large field and said he could see a mouse go by. I told him he had very good eyes. He looked at me in surprise and said, "They are big!... Wait, did I say mouse? I meant moose! I think Swedish in my head, but sometimes it comes out the wrong English". Leif is a wonderful person who loves all wildlife.

This book is also dedicated to my daughter, Jamie, and to my son, Jim.

Acknowledgments

This book would never have been published without the talent, commitment, and dedication of Patsy Jensen. Also, Kerry Kraha, who helped Patsy learn how to work Pixlr and edit the illustrations. Kerry and Patsy are both very talented artists. I also want to thank the writing group who meets at my home for all of their input, and Patsy's artist group The Painters in the Potting Shed. Thank you all for your advice, talent, and input. You made this book a reality for me.

Shirley Rogers Baustian

ABOUT THE ILLUSTRATOR

Pat (Mulligan) Jensen is a retired Clinical Therapist enjoying many facets of art in retirement. It wasn't until she returned to her roots in the Jefferson Valley of southwest Montana that she became " The Lovely and Beautiful Aunty Pat" known for telling virtually true tales through spirited animal puppets and colorful critter-doodles. With encouragement of a loving husband, family and friends she became " The Nana Girl" finding the secret to staying forever young through illustration.

A moose and a mouse went walking

in the forest dark and deep.

And as the mouse was talking

the moose began to weep.

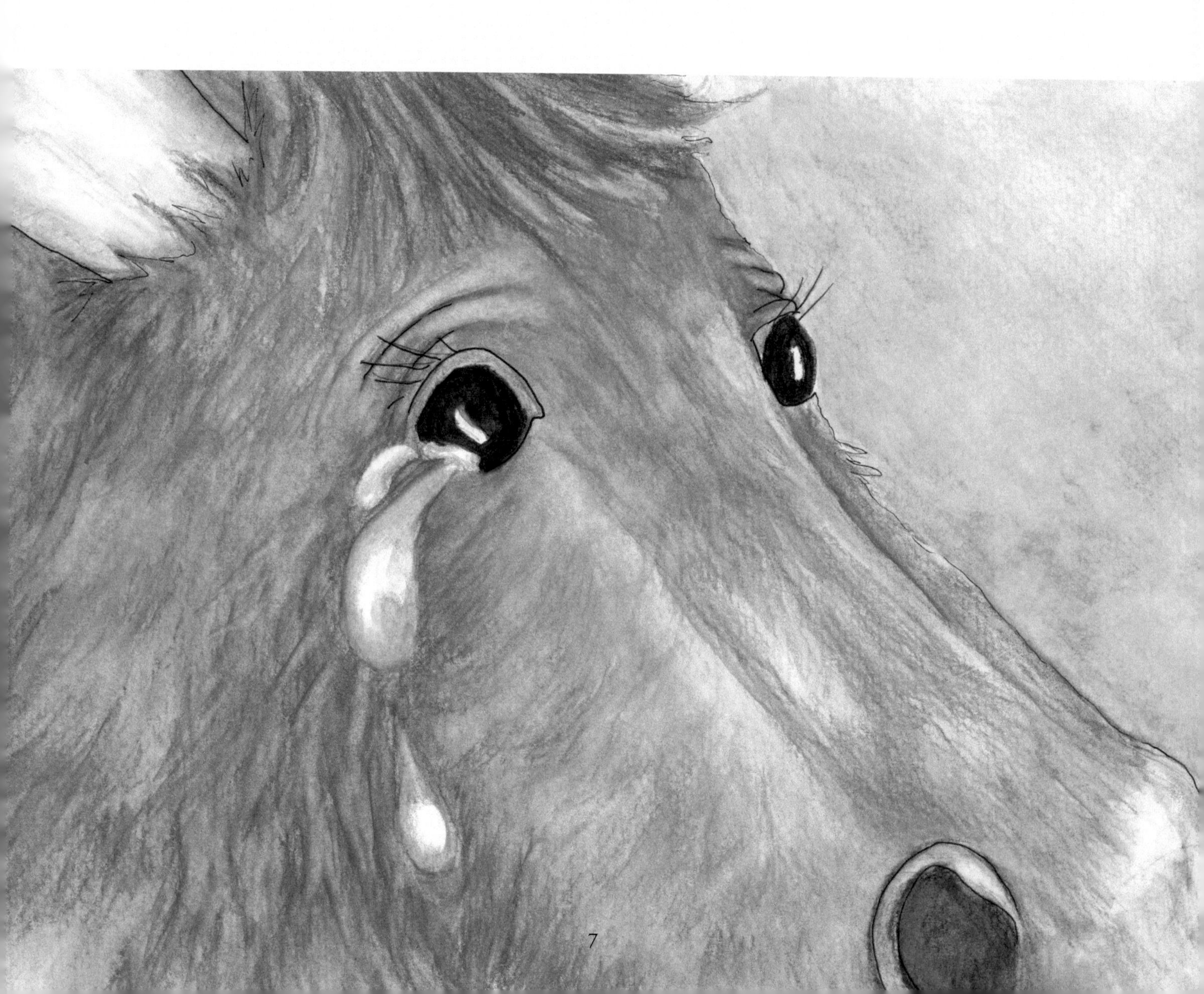

"What is it my friend?"

"Why this big tear?"

“Is there something in

the forest you fear?”

The moose looked down at his friend so small.

"Why I can hardly hear you at all!"

"Wait!" said the mouse.

I have a plan!"

"Lower your antlers,"

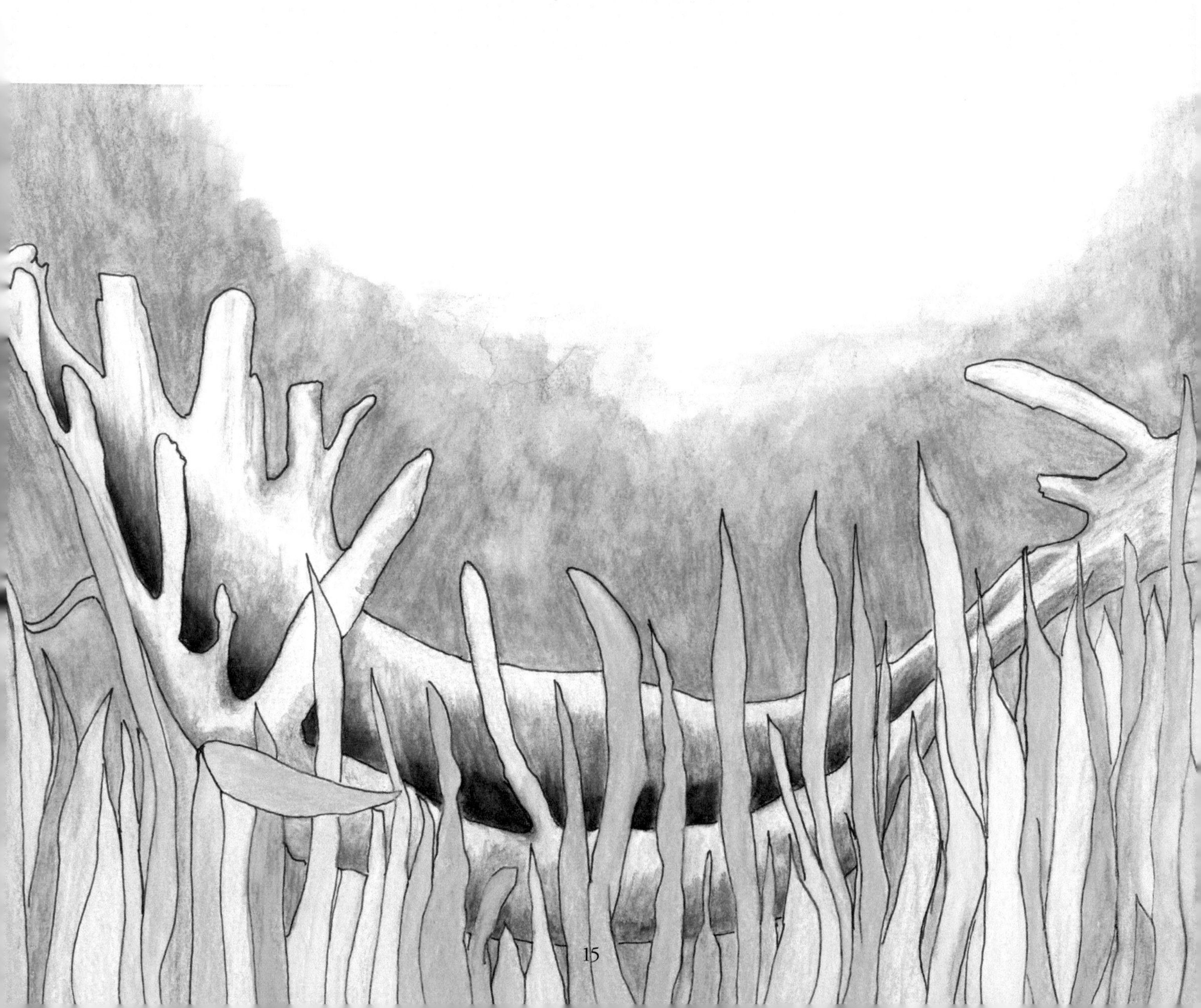

and up them, he ran.

The mouse sat down

next to his friend's big ear.

Now the mouse can ride and the moose can hear.

Printed in the United States
By Bookmasters